JN103505

五色の舟
Five-Colored Boat

津原泰水 * 作
Yasumi Tsuhara

宇野亞喜良 * 絵
Aquirax Uno

Toshiya Kamei * 英訳

五色の舟

Five-Colored Boat

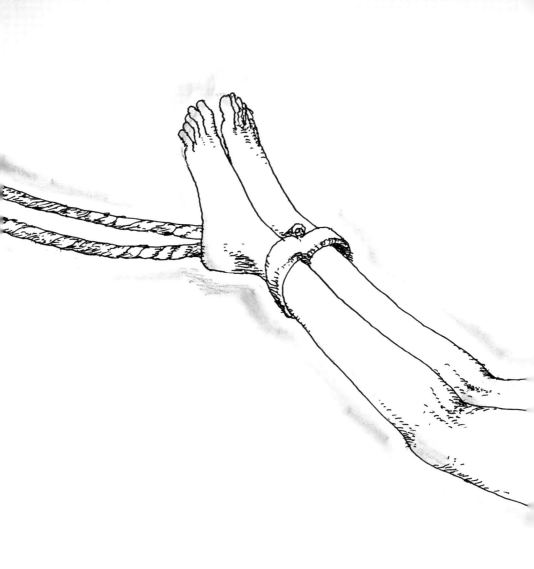

下駄屋に生まれたというくだんのために、僕らは一家総出で岩国に出向いた。

もちろん買い取るためだ。官憲からの申渡しで派手な興行ができなくなって久しかったが、秘かな催しに僕らを呼びつける旦那の数は、むしろ増えていた。国じゅうが惨憺（さんたん）たる状態にあって、生半可な涙や笑いが受けようはずもない。人々のまなざしを爛々とさせられるのは、もはや僕らのような、圧倒的に惨めな存在だけだった。

一夜の興行としては充分すぎる報酬をもらえたから、いつまで続くともつかない戦時にあって、僕らは未だ飢えていなかった。空襲への恐怖も薄かった。河に舫（もや）った舟で暮らしている僕らは、なにか起きたらすぐさま別の街へと逃げられるような心地でいた。

かりに飢えていたとしても、僕らのお父さんはなんとしてもくだんを買うべく算段したことだろう。そんな凄まじい怪物を一座に迎えられたなら、生きている間だけでも購入金の何倍、何十倍を稼ぎ出してくれるか知れない。死んだら死んだで骨だけの見世物にも、標本として商品にもなる。砕いて粉にすれば薬になるだろう。

When the news came that a cow had given birth to a kudan in a geta shop in Iwakuni, we set off on our journey. Of course, we had every intention of buying the man-faced ox.

The wartime authorities had banned us from putting on flashy performances a while ago. Even so, more patrons than ever before requested our presence at their private parties. With the whole country suffering extreme misery, no one had any interest in the lighter fare of tragedy and comedy. Only a wretched, mangled bunch like us could make the audience's eyes sparkle.

We were paid handsomely for a one-night gig, so we'd never faced starvation even in the midst of a seemingly endless war. The threat of air raids hardly concerned us. Since we lived on a boat anchored in the river, we felt we could flee to another town when push came to shove.

Even if we'd been starving, Father would have come up with a means of buying the kudan. With such a formidable monster in our troupe, we could triple, quadruple or even increase our investment tenfold while it was still alive. After its death, we could exhibit its bones and sell its parts as souvenirs. We could grind its remains into medicine, too.

もっとも、くだんは長くは生きないという噂に対して、それは（面倒見が悪いのだ）というのがお父さんの見解だった。（私は昭助も桜も死なせはしなかった）

一寸法師で怪力の昭助兄さんは、顔に濡れ紙を貼られた赤ん坊の死体としてお父さんの前に現れて、拾われた。当時のお父さんは、先を失った脚に義足として杖を縛りつけ、杖に縋って歩きながら、よく身投げの場所を探していた。ある晩、杖が折れて河原に転げ落ちて、大切な顔に怪我をした。捨て鉢になったお父さんは、すぐさまこの世におさらばするべく、水際に向かって蹲っていった。その途中、草陰に兄さんを見つけた。

乾きかけている紙を剝がしてやったが、赤ん坊は身じろぎひとつしなかった。木彫りの仏さんのようだった。愛らしさに思わず抱き上げ、そのずっしりした重みに驚いた。これは特別な子だと分かった。その身はすっかり冷たくなっていたけれど、ふたたび地べたに返す気がしなくなった。

6

Rumor had it that kudan were short lived. But Father opined that it would live longer with better care. "I didn't let Shosuke or Sakura die," he said.

Shosuke, my elder brother, was an issun-boshi. But despite his diminutive stature, he possessed great strength. Father had come across him as a foundling who had been left for dead with a wet sheet of paper covering his face. With an artificial leg tied to his knee stump and a cane in his hand, Father would often hobble along the river in search of a good spot to drown himself back in those days. One evening, his cane snapped into two, and he tumbled onto the riverbank, scratching his face—an actor's most valuable asset. Driven to despair, he crawled toward the water, ready to bid farewell to the world. There he found Shosuke among the grass.

Father removed the half-dry paper from his face, but the baby stayed still as a wooden Buddha statue. A wave of pity rushed over him, and he picked the baby up. The baby's weight took him by surprise. Father then realized he held a special baby in his arms. The baby's body felt cold to the touch, but Father refused to put him back on the ground.

Father held the baby close to his body, giving him warmth.

お父さんは思った。このまま朝まで暖め続けても息を吹き返さなければ、ともに水に入ろう。さきはこの子に導いてもらおう。もし息をしたなら、一緒にこちらに留まろう。

河原に朝の光が届いた瞬間、兄さんの身がびんと反り返った。

それからもお父さんの脱疽は進み、すでに切っていた脚の残りも、また反対の脚もほとんど失ってしまったけれど、自分から死ぬことは考えなくなった。僕らのよく知る、今のお父さんになっていった。

桜は、旧家の座敷牢で死にかけていた。噂を聞きつけたお父さんは、十三になっていた兄さんに背負われて、屋敷に通いつめた。そんな娘などいるか、とけんもほろろにされるほど、ここには必ずいると確信したそうだ。

塩をまかれながら半年も通って、今日はなにか家の気配がおかしいと感じていた晩、とつぜん対面をゆるされた。噂どおりの娘たちだった。しかし腰から下を分け合っていたもうひとりの桜は、すでに息をひきとっていた。

"If I can't revive him by the morning," Father mumbled. "I'll drown myself with him. He'll be my guide from now on. If he breathes again, I'll stay with him in this world."

When the morning sun reached the riverbank, Shosuke's body arched like a bow.

Father's gangrene progressively worsened over the years. He lost the remains of his leg stump and most of his other leg. Even so, he no longer thought about killing himself, and gradually became the person we knew so well today.

When Father heard of Sakura, she was dying and confined to her family's estate. Carried on the back of thirteen-year-old Shosuke, Father knocked on the door of the mansion many times.

"We don't have such a girl here!" her parents shouted.

The more they denied her existence, the more convinced Father became that the rumor was true.

Even though her parents threw salt at him, Father visited the mansion regularly for six months. One evening, something seemed out of the ordinary. He was allowed to meet Sakura for the first time. The rumor was true: two girls lay conjoined at the hips, one of them already dead.

（切り離さないと、もう片方も死ぬ）脱疽の経験から、そうお父さんは桜の両親に教えた。（この子を買わせてください。私が医者に診せます）

両親は首を縦にふらない。旧家の意地で血迷っている。子を売るくらいなら、いま目の前で死なせたいと思っている。

（では、もう死んだでいいではないですか。私が弔います。それとも、存在しなかった娘の葬式を出しますか。貴方がたに出せますか）

お父さんは自動車を呼ばせて、死んだ上半身がくっついたままの桜を蒲団袋（ふとんぶくろ）に詰め、犬飼先生の許に運んだ。せめて遺体としての体裁がととのえばいいとの条件で、先生は施術を引き受けた。死んだ側の上半身を切り離し、はみ出した内臓を縫い、たっぷりと膏薬を詰めて皮膚も縫った。

桜は生き延びた。骨の形がもうひとりが付いていた頃のままなので、前から見ると体がくの字に曲がっている。お父さんは桜の腰に、作りもののもうひとりを縛り付けてお客に覧（み）せようとしたが、彼女の芝居が下手で話にならなかった。

"We've got to separate them to save the other one," Father pleaded with the parents. "Please sell her to me. I'll take her to a doctor."

The parents refused. Their pride wouldn't allow them to consent to such a deal.

"She's not for sale. We'd rather let her die right here, right now."

"Then consider her dead already," Father continued. "I'll give her a proper funeral. Or can you bury her, a daughter who wasn't supposed to have existed?"

Father arranged a car, placed Sakura and her dead sister into a futon bag, and took her to Dr. Inukai. The doctor agreed to operate on her, reasoning that the least he could do was make the body presentable for a funeral. He cut off the dead upper part, put her internal organs back into her body, applied plenty of ointment to her incisions, and sewed her up.

Sakura survived. As her dead sister's bones had shaped her body, she looked bent like a dog's leg. Father tied a dummy to her hips and put her in a show, but it didn't work out because she was a terrible performer.

仕方なく体じゅうに鱗を描いて蛇女ということにして、蛙のまる呑みを覚えさせた。もちろんあとで吐き出すのだ。大抵、蛙はすでに死んでいるが、たまに生きたまま出てきて、跳ねて逃げていくのもいる。

こちらはうまくいって、今では桜の鱗は立派な彫り物で、お父さんや僕が毎度描きなおしてやる手間はない。

姿を現したあとは蛙を呑む以外にやることがなかった桜の、最近のもうひとつの大仕事は、別料金を払ったお客にまぐわいを見せることだ。お父さんは最初、昭助兄さんに抱かせようとした。ところが兄さんの一物が並外れて大きいものだから、ほとが裂けてしまった。そこで僕の仕事になった。

眺めるだけではなく自分で桜を抱きたがって、より大金をちらつかせるお客も少なくない。でもお父さんは決して頷かない。あとで桜が相手に似た子を産んでもしたら、具合が悪い。桜か僕か、それとも両方に似た子がいつか生まれるのを望んでいる。それなら一生、食べるに困らないから。

16

Instead, Father painted snake scales across her skin and dubbed her the Snake Woman. He taught her how to swallow a frog. Of course, she spit it out afterward. Most of the time, the frogs died inside her belly, but occasionally they came out alive and hopped away.

This worked fine. Eventually, Sakura got an impressive snakeskin tattooed all over her, so we didn't have to paint her before every show.

In addition to swallowing live frogs, Sakura put on a peep show for patrons who paid extra. At first, Father ordered Shosuke to sleep with her, but his enormous cock tore her vulva. Then Father assigned me to this task.

Many patrons weren't satisfied with just watching her. They flashed wads of cash, lusting after Sakura. But Father never accepted such a proposition. It'd be a terrible inconvenience if she got pregnant and gave birth to a baby who looked like the client. He wanted her to have a baby who looked like her or me. Then the child could make a living as part of our show.

物心がついたときには押入れの闇にいた僕の、最初の外の記憶は、河原を吹く風と、満天の星空と、生い茂った草の向こうで息をしているようにゆったりと沈んでは浮かぶ、大きな舟の影だ。そのときは、とても大きく見えた。

そこが新しい僕の世界だということはすぐに理解できたし、そう考えたとおり、朝になって僕を見つけたお父さんは、快く舟の上に導いてくれた。

お父さんは脚無しだが、僕は生まれつきの腕無しで、指は肩から生えている。でも自分と人との差異を意識しはじめたのは、お父さんの期待どおり見世物としてお客を喜ばせられるようになってからだ。なにしろ犬飼先生が気付くまで、家族も僕自身も、僕の耳が聞こえないのを知らなかったほどだ。ちゃんと命令が伝わるものだから、ただ極度に無口な子と思われていた。

僕は僕で、なんで桜は家族と喋らないのか、なぜ僕にだけはときたま、人とは違った調子で喋りかけてくるのか、不思議でならなかった。生まれてから長らく誰にも話しかけられなかった桜は、死んでしまったもうひとりとの間にしか通じない、特別な言葉を持っていた。それが分かるのは、音に関係なく生きている僕だけだった。

My childhood world was a dark, damp oshiire. My first memory was the shadow of a boat bobbing up and down, as if breathing behind thick veils of weeds and grasses under a starry sky. The boat seemed enormous to me back then.

I understood the boat was my new world. Just as I thought, Father led me to the boat when he found me in the morning.

Father had no legs. I was born without arms, fingers sprouting from my shoulders. Even so, I only became conscious of being different when I was able to entertain our audience as Father expected of me. Until Dr. Inukai examined me, no one, myself included, realized I was deaf. As I followed Father's instructions, he thought I was extremely quiet.

As for me, I wondered why Sakura didn't talk to the rest of our family, why she talked to me in a different way. As she had no one else to talk to ever since she was born, she'd developed a unique language to communicate with her dead twin. But when we met, I, who lived in my own soundless world, found I could also understand her.

僕らのいちばん新しい家族は、牛女の清子さんだ。みずから望んで舟に乗り込んできた。兄さんよりも年上で、世間をよく知っている。人と違うところをすこしは隠しておけたお蔭で、学校に通った経験さえあるのだ。

くだんのこともよく知っていて、それを一座に迎えるのを、ひどく嫌がっていた。本物の人と牛とのあいのこが来てしまった日には、本当は牛になんか似てやしない自分は、居場所を失うと思っている。

くだんは滅多に生まれないのだと、清子さんは教えてくれた。百年に一度だという。

牛だが人の顔をしていて、生まれつきよく喋るのだそうだ。

そして昔のことであれ未来のことであれ、本当のことしか言わないそうだ。

リャカーを牽いているのは、力持ちの昭助兄さんだ。荷台に敷かれた藁蒲団の上に、日除けの傘を差したお父さんと清子さんがいる。清子さんは膝の関節が後ろ前なので、長くは歩けない。

22

The last addition to our family was Kiyoko, the Cow Lady. She came aboard our boat of her own accord. Older than Shosuke, she was worldlier than the rest of us. As she was able to hide her differences to some degree, she'd even attended school.

She knew a lot about kudan and detested the idea of adding one to our troupe. She thought a creature that was half-human and half-ox would take her place in our show as she hardly resembled a cow.

According to Kiyoko, a kudan was born only once every hundred years.

An ox with the face of a man, it was born talkative.

And it spoke only the truth about the past and future.

* * *

Shosuke pulled the cart down the road. On the cart's bed, Father and Kiyoko were seated on a straw futon, holding parasols over their heads. Kiyoko's knees bent backward, so she couldn't walk for long.

彼女が元から牛に近いのはそこだけで、あとは犬飼先生に髪のなかに埋め込んでもらった角や、内をつなげた鼻の穴に通した縄や、啼き声や、ぶらぶらさせた大きな乳で、牛から生まれた人間のようなふりをするのだ。今は縄がなく、角も乳も膝も隠しているから、良家の奥さんが疲れて両脚を投げ出しているようにしか見えない。

かたわらを桜と僕が歩いている。僕はいつでも裸足だが、桜は、親切な旦那が買い与えてくれた革草履を誇らしげにしている。この旦那は桜のことを本当に好いていて、蛇女でもいいから妾にしたいと持参金までさげてきた。お父さんは断り、あとで僕らにこう言った。（私たちをまるごと買い取らないかぎり、小屋のなかでの幻は手に入らないよ。それをあの方はご存じない）

清子さんはリャカーの上で、まだお父さんを説得しようとしている。（くだんは気味が悪いわ。未来も言い当てるのよ。お前は死ぬまで貧乏だとか、いつごろ死ぬって教えられるかもしれないのに、そんなことにお金を払うお客がいると思う？）

（たくさんいるだろうね）

That was the only cow-like characteristic she was born with. She pretended to be a woman born of a cow, mooing on all fours —Dr. Inukai had implanted horns in her forehead, a rope through her nose ring, and augmented her breasts so they hung down like cow udders. Now with her horns, knees, and breasts hidden, she looked like a respectable housewife.

Sakura and I walked along beside them. I was always barefoot, but Sakura proudly wore a pair of leather zori, a gift from a kind-hearted patron. This patron was truly fond of Sakura. He even offered to buy her and make her his concubine, saying that he didn't care if she was a snake woman. Father turned him down.

"He can't own the illusion from our shack unless he buys all of us," Father told us later. "That man doesn't realize that."

On the cart, Kiyoko tried to talk Father out of buying the kudan.

"Oh, it gives me the creeps!" Kiyoko said. "It can foretell the future. It may tell you you'll die poor. Who would pay for that, Father?"

"Many, actually."

和に
郎や
さ桜

父きん　と　清子

照助

（じゃあお父さんは、自分がいつ死ぬと知ったら嬉しいの）

（目前のこととして言われたなら動揺はするだろうが、聞かねば良かったとは思うまいね。清子をからかっているんじゃないんだよ。私に自分の寿命が分かれば、お前たちに遺すべきものを、どのくらいの間に準備すればいいかも分かるじゃないか）

夏の遠出は一苦労だ。とりわけ僕と桜は、見世物としての価値を下げないよう、どんなに暑くとも一張羅を着込んで、僕はただ懐手をしているように、桜は肌を見せぬようにしていないといけない。そのうえリヤカーまで重いときに、僕らの歩みはひどく遅かった。朝のうちに出立したにもかかわらず、岩国までには野宿をはさまねばならず、やっと街場に着いたのは、翌日の昼近くだった。

お父さんと兄さんだけなら半分の時間で済んだろうに、それでもお父さんが一家総出を望んだのは、内心ではどこか、くだんを怖がっていたのだろうと今にして思う。だから、たとえ買えるとなっても、最後の答は全員で出したかったのではないかと。

"Then Father," Kiyoko continued. "Would you want to know when you'll die?"

"I may be upset if I was told I would die soon," Father answered. "But I wouldn't regret knowing my future. I'm not making fun of you, Kiyoko. If I knew when I'd die, I'd know how long I had to leave you what you need."

It was troublesome to travel a long distance in summertime. Despite the summer heat, Sakura and I covered ourselves with our best kimono in order to protect our value as roadshow spectacles. I pretended to have hands inside my sleeves. Sakura hid her skin beneath the fabric. On top of that, the heavy cart slowed our gait. Even though we left in the morning, we had to spend the night in a clearing. We arrived in town at noon the following day.

If Father and Shosuke had traveled alone, it would have taken them half the time. But for some reason, Father wanted to bring all of us with him. Perhaps he was subconsciously afraid of the kudan. Maybe he wanted us to have a say in his decision to buy the creature.

下駄屋が乳を採るために大切にしてきた牝牛が、種牛を乗せてもいないのに急に産んだのだと聞いた。（きっと下駄屋の親爺か若いのが、種を入れたんだろう）とお父さんは笑う。それでくだんを産ませたのだとしたら、大したお手柄だ。

乞食に教えてもらった坂道を上っていくと、それらしき一軒の前に、軍の自動車が連なっているのが見えてきた。帆布で荷台を被ったトラックもあり、けっこうな数の軍人や軍属がそれらの間を行き来している。

（さきを越された。くだんは軍に持っていかれる）そう口惜しそうに叫んだお父さんだったが、やがて吐息をもらして、（未来を予言するというのだから、考えてみれば無理もない。大枚を叩いたあとで接収されるよりはましか。幸運だったと思うことにしよう）

（お父さん、犬飼先生だ）兄さんが叫んで、（あそこ、あそこ）と指を差す。

（先生）（犬飼先生）僕らは懸命に坂を上がった。追い払おうと、下士たちが迫ってくると、かえって盛んに、（先生、先生）（犬飼さま！）

30

According to the rumors, the geta maker's treasured milk cow had given birth without mating with a stud bull.

"The geta maker or his son must have mated with the cow," Father said, laughing. "If he knocked it up that way, it'd be a great feat."

We climbed the hill a beggar had indicated, and our destination came into view. There was a row of military vehicles parked in front of the geta shop, including a flatbed truck whose load was covered with a tarpaulin. Several uniformed soldiers and civilian employees moved around them.

"They beat us to it! They're taking the kudan away!" Father cried. "Of course, they want it," Father sighed. "After all, it foretells the future. It could have been worse. It'd have been worse if they had confiscated it from us after we'd paid a fortune. We should consider ourselves lucky."

"Father, look," Shosuke shouted. "That's Dr. Inukai! Look. There." He pointed.

"Doctor! Dr. Inukai!" We climbed the hill with all our might. Some privates walked toward us with menacing intent. "Doctor! Doctor!" We cried louder. "Dr. Inukai!"

こちらに気付いた先生が、（患者だ）と叫びながら下士たちを追い越した。普通の人は罹らない病気に悩まされがちな僕らを、ほかの患者がいないときに限られるものの、快く診てくれる先生だ。今は、元々の専門だった黴菌への知識を買われ、兵器補給廠の研究室に勤めている。

兵隊たちの手前だからか、その日の先生は芝居がかって見えるほど厳めしかった。（どうしてここに君たちがいる。なにをしに来た）

（くだんを買いに来たのです）とお父さんが答える。

（あれは噂に過ぎない。諦めて帰りたまえ）

（ではあのトラックは？）

（特別なものは乗っていない。不要な牛を実験用に買い取っただけだ）

（分かりました、そう納得いたします）そうお父さんは頷いたものの、相手への気易さから微笑まじりに、（犬飼さま、ひとつだけ教えてください、くだんは本当に喋るのですか）

（私に分かるか）と、先生は冷水を浴びせるように返してきた。（そんな生き物は世に存在しないというのに）

Dr. Inukai noticed us.

"They're my patients," Dr. Inukai yelled, overtaking the privates. He attended to us when other patients weren't around as we tended to suffer from rare ailments. Originally trained as a germ expert, he now worked at the ordnance depot's laboratory.

The doctor looked theatrically stern and dignified in front of the soldiers.

"What are you doing here? Why are you here?" the doctor asked.

"We've come to buy the kudan," Father answered.

"I'm afraid you're on a wild goose chase. You should give up and go home."

"But what is that truck doing here?"

"Nothing out of the ordinary. We've purchased an unwanted cow for medical research."

"I see." Father nodded and then flashed a smile as he usually did. "Dr. Inukai, please tell me one thing. Does the kudan really talk?"

"How should I know?" Dr. Inukai said in a cold, dismissive tone. "There's no such creature."

お父さんは唇をむすんで先生を見つめた。先生も見つめ返した。

（そうでした）

お父さんが引き下がると、先生はようやっと表情をゆるめて、

（ここまで来られたのだから、みな体調は悪くないようだ）

（お蔭さまで）

（道中、気をつけて帰りたまえ）

……土埃を巻き上げてトラックが坂を下っていく。犬飼先生を乗せた自動車もそれに続き、居残っていた下士や軍属も走り去った。見送っていた主人や家人たちが、門口を閉ざしはじめる。

（本当のところはどうなんだって、あの人たちに訊いてみようか）兄さんがお父さんを振り返る。

（どうせ口止めされているだろう）

僕らもまた、坂道を下りはじめた。またこれまでどおりの日々に帰っていくのだ。お父さんの落胆は察しながらも、正直なところ僕はほっとしていた。

Father closed his mouth and stared at the doctor. The doctor stared back.

"Yes, of course." Father relented, averting his gaze. The doctor relaxed his expression.

"You walked all the way here," the doctor said. "You must be in good shape."

"Thanks to you, doctor."

"Have a safe journey home."

The truck rumbled down the hill, raising clouds of dust in its wake. The car carrying Dr. Inukai followed close behind. After a while, the privates and the civilian employees also left. The geta maker and his servants sent them off. After the cars were gone, they closed the gates.

"Why don't we ask them?" Shosuke said, glancing toward Father.

"No, they won't tell us anything."

We, too, went down the hill. We were going home empty-handed. Even though Father was visibly disappointed, I felt relieved.

くだんは得られそうもないとなり、気持ちに余裕の生まれた清子さんが、さっきまでとは一変、その姿を拝めなかったことを残念がっている。（いくら兵隊さんたちの手前とはいえ、犬飼先生の態度は変だった。やっぱりあのトラックに乗っていたのよ。私たちが苦労してやって来たのは分かってるんだから、後学のために覗かせてくれても良さそうなものじゃない）

（後学って、清子はくだんから何を教わりたかったんだい）とお父さん。

（ふるまいや声や、いくらでも為になるわ。本物のあいのこなんだから）

（そういう話か。私はまた、お前も自分の寿命を知りたいのかと思ったよ）

（それは御免）

（たとえくだんを買えたとしても、私と桜以外は近付かせないつもりだった。桜なら、くだんの言葉も通じないだろうからね）

（和ちゃんにも聞えないわ）

（和郎は最も遠ざけないといけない。声が聞えなくとも人がなにを言っているのか解る子なんだから、くだんと目が合っただけでも、きっとおかしくなってしまうよ）

38

Now that the kudan was out of our reach, Kiyoko became cheerful.

"I wish I could have taken a peek at it!" she said. "Did you notice how strangely the doctor behaved in front of the soldiers, Father? The kudan must have been on that truck! He must've known we'd come all this way. He should've let us take a look at it. I could've learned something!"

"What did you want to learn, Kiyoko?" Father asked.

"Well, how it behaves, how it talks. Anything would've helped me. It's the genuine article, after all."

"Oh, that's what you meant," Father said. "I thought you also wanted to know when you'd die."

"No thank you!"

"Even if I'd been able to buy it, I wouldn't have let any of you near the kudan," Father continued. "Except for Sakura. She wouldn't understand the kudan."

"Neither does Kazu-chan," Kiyoko said.

"Kazuo should stay away, too," Father insisted. "He understands people without hearing their voices, so he'd go crazy just by meeting its gaze."

このお父さんの言葉に、僕は震え上がった。本当にトラックにくだんが乗って

いたんだとしたら、これは大変なことになったと思った。

お父さんが犬飼先生と話している最中、僕はちらちら、トラックの荷台へと視

線を向けていた。なにとはなし、呼ばれているような気がしたのだ。格別な呼ば

れ方ではなくて、知らない人から不意に（腕無し）とか（化け物）と呼ばれたと

きのような、つまり僕にとっては普通な感じだった。

帆布の薄い隙間に、荷台を囲むあおり板が覗いている。内には檻でも収まって

いるのか、ただ黄色っぽい薄闇だけがあった。何度も見直しているうち、ふと、

その闇が濃くなった。確かだ。

それでいて、小さな水たまりのような一点だけが、外の光を撥ね返していた。

本当に乗っていたのなら、僕を見ているくだんの眼だったことになる。

それが続くほど、くだんの仕業に違いないという確信は深まった。

僕は同じような夢ばかりみるようになった。くだんとは無関係な夢だったが、

His words made me shiver. If the kudan was truly on the truck, it could spell trouble.

While Father was chatting with the doctor, I repeatedly glanced toward the tarpaulin-covered load of the truck. Someone seemed to be calling me. It didn't feel like anything out of the ordinary. It felt normal, as if some stranger called me "armless boy" or "monster."

A board had peeked through the gaps in the tarpaulin. Beyond the wood, there seemed to be a cage. Only yellowish darkness was visible. As I kept glancing, the darkness deepened.

Within that darkness, like a puddle at night, a dot reflected the light seeping in from outside.

Perhaps that was the kudan's eye observing me.

* * *

I dreamed the same dream over and over again. My dream had nothing to do with the kudan. Even so, as the dream persisted, I became increasingly certain it was the kudan's doing.

海の夢だった。兄さんや桜と浅蜊や石蓴を採りにいく、いつもの海岸ではなく、ずっと沖合の夢だ。

家族はみな舟上にいる。半開きにされた雨除けの被いの向こうには、低い曇り空、黒ずんだ波、そして白い泡。どの方角を向いても同じ景色だった。僕らは舟ごと、海原を漂っている。

どこか遠くを目指しているようだが、僕らの舟に帆を掛ける柱はなく、誰かが漕いでいる様子もない。ひたすら波まかせの、いつどう終わるとも知れない舟旅の途上に、僕らはいた。

遠い波間にふと、こちらと似たような舟影が現れる。（ほかの舟だ）（舟？）とみな驚いて被いの外に顔を突き出す。とても珍しい事態らしい。

さらに波の悪戯か、舟同士が急接近する。ともに急な川でも下っているかのように、相手はみるみる迫ってくる。いざ間近にすると、こちらより遥かに立派な舟だ。長さも幅も倍はありそうだ。

My recurring dream started off at sea. With Sakura and Shosuke, I sailed further offshore than usual to gather clams and sea lettuce.

All of us were on the boat. Beyond the half-open tarpaulin, the landscape looked the same in every direction: the downcast gray sky, dark waves, and white foam. Our boat drifted with the current.

We headed toward some faraway place, but we had neither mast nor sails. Nor did anyone row. We were on a seemingly endless voyage at the mercy of the waves.

A boat similar to ours emerged from the distant waves.

"Another boat!"

"Boat?" Surprised, the rest of my family poked their heads outside the tarpaulin.

The other boat sped toward us, closing in the distance. At closer range, the other boat impressed me. It was twice the width and length of our boat.

激突を避けるべく、昭助兄さんが竹竿を構えて舳先に立つ。二艘はなお距離を縮め、とうとう兄さんの竹竿がつっかえる。竿が激しく撓る。兄さんが跳ね飛ばされやしまいかと、僕は心配になる。

（なに、滅多にあることじゃないさ）竿と格闘しながらも、兄さんはこの椿事を楽しんでいるようだ。

（こんなに近付くなんてねえ）と清子さんが歌うように言う。

先方の船頭が、なにかをこちらに投げようとしているのに気付いて、僕も雨除けから出ていく。投げ込まれてみれば襤褸にくるまれた石で、それに赤い縄を縛り付けてある。ぶつかって舟が破損する前に、引き合って互いを繋留しようという提案だろう。

僕は縄を足で押さえ込み、口で結び目をほどきはじめる。繋留を手伝ってくれるのだと思い、僕は場所を空ける。お父さんが壁ってくる。

46

In his attempt to avoid collision with the other boat, Shosuke stood on the bow with a bamboo pole in his hand. As the distance narrowed, his pole struck the other boat and became bent.

"Careful," I said. "Watch out."

"Nah, it's no big deal." Even though Shosuke struggled with the pole, he seemed to enjoy the incident.

"We've never been close to another boat," Kiyoko singsonged.

The boatman motioned to throw something toward us. I stepped out from under the tarpaulin. A stone wrapped in a rag landed on our boat. A red rope was tied around the stone. The boatman intended to keep a distance between the boats before we crashed into each other.

I held the rope with my feet and tried to untie the knot with my teeth.

Father crawled toward me. I made room for him, thinking he'd help me.

僕の予想ははずれる。お父さんは手早く縄をほどくや、その端で自分の身を縛ってしまう。（今を逃）したら、こんな機は二度と巡ってこない）

　一瞬、お父さんは僕に笑いかける。それから海に飛び込む。舟同士がまた離れはじめる。

　新しい舟に引き上げられていくお父さんを見つめながら、僕は、またこうなってしまった、と嘆息する。しばらく泣く。別の夢では清子さんが、また別の夢では昭助兄さんが、同じようにして海に飛び込んだ。そして新しい舟に引き上げられるのだった。

　夢には、より奇妙な続きがある。相手の舟影が波間に消えてしまうまで見つめたあと、僕がしょんぼりと雨除けの下に戻っていくと、そこにはちゃんと家族全員が揃っている。ほかの舟とぶつかりかけたことなど嘘のように、それ以前となんら変わらぬ、物静かな風情で。

　さっきのは、どこか余所の世界での出来事だったらしい。僕はそう納得して、ほっとする。かといって去っていったほうの家族のことも、忘れてはいない。忘れられるはずがない。

To my surprise, Father quickly untied the rope and then tied it to himself.

"Here's the chance of a lifetime," Father said. "I can't miss it." He flashed a smile and dove into the sea. The distance between the boats widened.

As I watched Father being pulled out of the water and onto the other boat, I sighed. "Here we go again." I sobbed for a while. Some nights, Shosuke or Kiyoko dove into the sea in a similar fashion before they were pulled out of the water by the other boat.

Then my dream took an odd turn. After the other boat disappeared among the waves, I went back under the tarpaulin and found my whole family there. They had serene looks on their faces as if nothing had happened.

It hit me that all of this might have happened in another dimension. I was relieved. Even so, my mind returned to my family who had leaped into the sea. There was no way I'd forget them.

僕は夢を数えていた。四十九回続いて、この明け方には五十回めをみるのだろうと思っていた月の明るい晩、不意に犬飼先生が僕らの舟を訪れた。

（夜分に失礼するよ。雪之助をお借りしたい）

お父さんのことだ。脱疽にかかる以前は旅芝居の花形だった。そして犬飼先生はその時代、一番の御贔屓だったのだそうだ。京都より西の興行なら、必ず初日に駆けつけてくれたという。

先生の態度には、岩国で会ったときの厳めしさとはまた違う、どこか悲しげな重苦しさが漂っていた。（折り入っての話がある。ちょっと医院まで来てもらえまいか。上に車を待たせてある）

（診察でしょうか）

（そうではない。ただ話をするだけだ）

（では、いまここで済ませてはいただけませんか）すでに眠りかけていたお父さんは、外出を億劫がった。（もしご内密なら、子供たちは小屋の方へ払います）

50

* * *

The same dream had come to me forty-nine times in a row. The night Dr. Inukai paid us an unannounced visit, a bright moon shone overhead. I expected to have the dream for the fiftieth time at dawn.

"Excuse me for disturbing you so late. Let me talk to Yukinosuke." Back when Father was still a top-billed actor in his traveling troupe, Dr. Inukai was his number one fan. He never failed to attend the opening day performance whenever Father's troupe toured west of Kyoto.

When we'd first met him in Iwakuni, Dr. Inukai carried himself rather stiffly. Now he looked sad and serious.

"We must talk. Can you come to the clinic? I have a cab waiting."

"For a checkup?"

"No. I just want to talk."

"Can we talk here?" Already half-asleep, Father was reluctant to go out. "If you need privacy, I'll send my children to the shack."

興行に必要な資材や道具は、近くの橋の下の掘建て小屋にしまってある。僕らの別宅といったところだが、河が増すと床上まで水が上がってくるので、寝泊まりには向かない。

（無理をさせたくはないのだが）先生はちらりと僕を見た。（和郎はどのくらいの距離までなら、その）

（人の心を読めるか、でございますか）

（うん）

（私にも見当がつきません。傍にいるものと思い込んで呼びかけたら、河原から上がってくることもあります。しかし口もきけませんし、読み書きもできませんから、誰に伝わる気遣いもございません）

お父さんはそう言ったが、本当は桜とだったら話せる。隠しているつもりはなかった。ふたりとも周囲にそう説明できないだけだった。

先生はかぶりを振って、（やはり来てもらいたい）

（昭助は同行させても？ さもないと犬飼さまにおぶっていただくことに）

（同行は構わないが、話の間は外で待たせてほしい）

お父さんは了承し、留守を頼もうとして清子さんを呼んだ。どこからも返事がない。こっそり出掛けてしまったようだ。お父さんは僕に留守番を頼んで、寝入っていた昭助兄さんを揺り起こした。

52

We stored props for performances in the shack under a bridge nearby. It was our second home, but we didn't sleep there because the floor was flooded when the water levels rose.

"I hate to force you to do this," the doctor said and glanced at me. "How potent is Kazuo's…"

"His mind-reading ability?"

"Yes."

"I have no idea. Sometimes I call his name thinking he's beside me, but he actually comes from the riverbank. But he can't talk or read or write, so he won't tell anyone."

In reality, I could talk to Sakura. I never meant to hide it from anyone. It was just that neither of us could explain it to the others.

"You must come with me," the doctor insisted.

"May Shosuke accompany me? Otherwise you'd have to carry me on your back."

"He may, but he must wait outside while we talk."

Father nodded and called Kiyoko. But there was no reply. She seemed to have slipped away. Father asked me to look after the house and shook Shosuke awake.

兄さんは生返事をして雨除けの外に出ていき、河に小便をしてから戻ってきた。

お父さんを背負ってからも、はんぶん眠っているように見えた。

三人が舟を降りて河原を横切り、土手を上がっていくのを、僕はじっと見送った。

「和郎さん」

呼びかけられて振り向くと、とうに眠ったものと思っていた桜が、頭を起こしてこっちを見ていた。

「お父さん、ほかの舟に乗ってしまう？」

そのとき悟った。桜もまた、僕と同じ夢をみ続けてきたことを。桜もくだんと目が合ったのだ。

僕は舟から飛び出し、土手を駆け上がった。すぐ下の道路に、走り去っていく自動車のランプが見えた。追い付くべくもない灯りを追って、僕は夜道を駆けた。

裸も同然の格好だったが、そんなことは忘れていた。

いま引き留めなかったら、お父さんはほかの舟に移ってしまう。そのあとも僕らの舟に姿を留めてくれるかもしれないが、それはもはや、これまでのお父さんではないのだ。

Shosuke gave a half-hearted answer, went out of the tarpaulin, and urinated into the river before he returned. Still half asleep, he carried Father on his back.

I watched as the three of them got off the boat, walked across the riverbank, and climbed the embankment.

"Kazuo." I heard a voice and turned around. Sakura raised her face and looked at me. I thought she'd been asleep.

"Is Father boarding another boat?"

It was then I realized she'd dreamed the same dream I had. Sakura, too, had met the kudan's gaze.

I leaped out of the boat and ran up the embankment. A car sped along the road below. I saw its tail lights moving farther away. I ran through the night, chasing the lights. I was half-naked, but I didn't care.

If I didn't stop him now, he'd get on another boat. His shell might stay on our boat afterward, but that wouldn't be the same.

出版のご案内

史上最悪の
渋谷テロ事件から2年
犯罪は、連鎖する――。

秦 建日子

チェンジ・ザ・ワールド
Change the World

ページをめくる手が
止まらない！

映画化されたベストセラー
『And so this is Xmas
サイレント・トーキョー』に続く **衝撃作！**

●予価1870円（税込） ISBN 978-4-309-03094-4

河出書房新社　〒151-0051 東京都渋谷区千駄ヶ谷
tel:03-3404-1201 http://www.k

Change the World

秦建子

▼一八七〇円

「おめでとう。君が世界を変えるんだ」
──最悪の渋谷テロ事件から一年半。あの日の悪夢が、甦る……本所南署の新コンビ・世田志乃夫と天羽史が繰り広げるノンストップ・クライムサスペンス!

私小説

金原ひとみ編著 尾崎世界観/西加奈子/島田雅彦/町屋良平/しいきともみ/エリイ/千葉雅也/水上文

作家は真実の言葉で嘘をつく──。どこまでが「私」で、どこからが「小説」なのか? 第一線の表現者たちが物語の片たなリアルを拓く。話題沸騰の「文芸」特集に書下しを加えた決定版。

▼

スキャンダルによって落ち

五色の舟

Goshiki no Fune

犬飼医院の位置は分かっている。自動車を見失ってからは、思いつくかぎりの近道をとった。月の下を駆け抜けていく腕の無い影に、通行者は足を竦め、自動車は急停止した。どこか誇らしい思いが胸に満ちはじめる。誰しもが足を止めるのは、僕が特別な子供だからだ。

特別な子供が、特別なお父さんのために走っているからだ。

医院の玄関先に人影は見えなかった。庭に入り、隣家とを隔てる木塀が照らされている箇所を見出して、その隙間に入っていく。あかりは間違いなく、お父さんの気配を含んでいた。

（和郎じゃないか）と後ろから呼ばれて、身を竦める。昭助兄さんだった。（急患かと思って灯籠の陰に隠れていたよ。追いかけてきたのか。どうした）

僕は窓の下まで、ぴょんぴょんと後退って見せた。人を招くときの合図である。

（覗きたいのか）

頷く。

I knew where the clinic was located. After I lost sight of the car, I took a short cut through the back alleys. Passersby froze and cars screeched to a halt as they saw an armless figure dashing in the moonlight. An odd sort of pride filled my chest. They stopped because I was different. Because I was a different boy running for his different father.

There was no one at the entrance to the clinic. I slipped through a gap in the wooden fence and entered the yard. I detected Father's presence in the light seeping through the window.

"Is that you, Kazuo?" A voice came from behind me, and I cringed. It was Shosuke. "I thought you were an emergency patient, so I was hiding behind a stone lantern. What are you doing here?"

I jumped backward toward the window, gesturing for him to join me.

"Are you going to peek inside?"

I stood on tiptoe and tried to peek through the window.

（見つかるなよ。俺まで叱られるから）

兄さんも窓の下に来た。差し出された掌に足を掛け、その肩に上がる。

診察室の続きの、犬飼先生の居室だった。僕がちょうど見下ろせる位置に長椅子があり、先生とお父さんが、後ろ向きに隣り合っている。

（とどのつまり、どういう生き物であると、犬飼さまはお考えなので？）

（分からない。私の知識の及ぶ範囲ではない）

（では、それこそ、真実しか語らないというくだんならば、問えば正直に教えてくれるのではありませんか）

（もちろん何度も訊いたし、説明もされた。しかし話の基底が違いすぎて、論理的に理解するのが難しいのだ。無理に私たちの科学で割り切ろうとすれば、牛に寄生している何らかに過ぎない、ということになろう。しかしそれが学習してもいない人語で、我々の歴史の仔細を語る、まったく未知の現象ということになり、所詮は謎だらけだ）

（そんな謎めいた獣の言い分を、軍の上層は真剣に信じているのですね）

"Don't let them see you, or you'll get us both in trouble."

Shosuke joined me under the window. He extended his hands. I placed one foot on his cupped palms and climbed onto his shoulder.

I saw the living room adjacent to the examination room. Below me, Dr. Inukai and Father were seated on a couch with their backs toward me.

"Doctor, what kind of creature do you think it is?"

"I've got no idea. It's beyond my expertise."

"The kudan only tells the truth. Will it give you an honest answer if you ask it?"

"Of course, I've asked it many times, and it's answered me each time. But it makes little logical sense to us because it's completely outside of our knowledge base. As far as our science is concerned, it's merely a parasitic entity within an ox. But it talks of human history in detail, in human language, without having studied it. The creature is full of mysteries."

"How can the military give credence to what such a strange creature says?"

（鵜呑みではない。くだんの弁には上層部しか知らぬ事実が、あまりにも多く含まれているのだ。この世界の未来を知るからこそ、まるで千里眼のように、いまどこで何が起きているのか悟れるというわけだ）

（たとえば、たとえばですが、上層部に曲者がいて、周囲を意の儘にするため、からくりを弄しているといった可能性は）

（何度も言ってきたとおり、くだんは確かに生きている。心臓は鼓動し、糞も小便も垂れ、怪我をすれば血を流す。そんなからくりが作れるものか）

（何を食べるのですか）

（仔牛と同じだ。牛の乳をやたらと欲しがる。あとは大概、鼾をかいて眠っている）

（その同じ口が、やがて本土に恐るべき爆弾が落ちると言っているのですね、都市がまるごと消えてしまうような。そして日本は負けると）

（あくまでこの世界での話だ。すでに上層のほとんどが補給廠を訪れ、くだんに導かれて別の世界に逃げていったよ、日本が勝ち残る世界に。私もそろそろ腹を括るべきかと思う。次にお前と会うとき、今と同じ私であるという自信はない）

64

"They can't completely. But the kudan has recounted too many facts known only to the top brass. It can tell the future of mankind. Like a clairvoyant, it knows what's happening in the world."

"Perhaps the military created a mechanism to manipulate those around them. Is such a thing possible?"

"As I've told you many times, the kudan is alive. Its heart is beating. It urinates and defecates. It bleeds when injured. It's impossible to make such a device."

"What does it eat?"

"Like a calf, it loves cow milk. When it's not drinking, it's asleep and snoring."

"But it's saying a terrible bomb will be dropped on Japan, annihilating a whole city? And Japan will lose the war?"

"Only in the Japan of this world. Most military leaders have visited the ordnance depot and escaped to another world. Maybe it's also time for me to leave for a world where Japan wins the war. Next time you see me, I can't say it'll still be the same me."

（そこが分からないのでございます。犬飼さまが別の世界にお逃げになったとして、でも相変わらずこちらの世界にも犬飼さまはおられる。さっきそう仰有った。いったいそれで、犬飼さまの世界が変わったということになるのでしょうか）

（心の置きどころの問題、と、そう解釈しているよ。こう例えたらどうだろう。雪之助が脱疽に罹らず、花形でい続けられた世界があるとしよう。想像してみることはあろうね。そちらこそ本当の自分であって、脱疽のこちらは幻に過ぎないと、もしお前が確信できたなら、あとはそれこそ夢のなかにいるように、怪我をしても病気をしても痛くも苦しくもない。かりそめと思える痛み苦しみを、人は深刻には捉えないものだ。死も恐ろしくない。死んだら、次は本当の自分として目覚めるのだろうから）

（なにごとも気の持ちよう。そういうお話にしか、私には聞えません）

（私にだってそう聞える。しかしくだんがそう語るのだ、人智を超えた存在が。雪之助、この世界は過酷なうえ、医術にも限界がある。私はなんとしてでも、どの世界ででも、お前を長く生かしたい）

（くだんは、確かに導いてくれるのですか）

（私は信じる。信じることにした）

雪之助、この世界は過酷なうえ、医術にも限界がある。私はなんとしてでも、どの世界ででも、お前を長く生かしたい）先生はお父さんを抱き寄せた。

66

"That's how you lose yourself, Dr. Inukai. Even if you escape to another world, another version of you remains in this world. Can you say your world has changed?"

"That depends on your perspective. Let's suppose there's another world where you never suffered gangrene and still perform on stage. You must've imagined that. You may say that's really you. The one who suffered gangrene is an illusion. If you can be sure of that, you wouldn't mind getting injured or sick. You wouldn't take temporary pain so seriously. You wouldn't fear death either. If you die, you'll wake as the real you."

"Everything depends on perspective. Is that what you're saying?"

"That's what we hear from the kudan, a creature beyond human intellect, Yukinosuke. This world is cruel, and medicine is limited. No matter where I am, I want to make you live longer." The doctor held Father in his arms.

"Will the kudan lead us to another world?"

"I believe so. I've decided to believe."

先生はお父さんに接吻しはじめ、あとはまともな会話を成さなかった。居た堪れなくなった僕は、兄さんの肩から飛び降りた。

やはり僕と桜は、くだんから何かを受け取ったらしい。窓の向こうのやりとりには分からない言葉も多々あったが、大筋は理解できた。それでいて驚きを感じなかったのは、すでに僕らが別なかたちで、その内容を知っていたからだ。

お父さんを待たねばならない兄さんを残して、僕はふたたび河まで走った。いざ辿り着くと、舟の上に戻るのが怖くなった。きっと桜は起きたまま、僕の報告を待っていることだろう。最悪の結果を報告する勇気が、僕にはまだなかった。

舟の横を行き過ぎ、橋の下の掘建て小屋に向かった。しばらくその内に籠もって、気持ちを整理したかった。帰ってきたお父さんと兄さんが僕を探すとして、最初に覗いてみるのはあの小屋だろう。だからたとえ寝入ってしまっても、余計な心配をかけずに済む。

The doctor was now busy kissing Father. Having seen enough, I climbed down from Shosuke's shoulders.

Sakura and I seemed to have received some kind of communication from the kudan. Despite some unfamiliar words, I'd understood the gist of Dr. Inukai and Father's conversation. Even so, the story didn't come as a surprise because Sakura and I had learned of it another way.

I said goodbye to Shosuke, left the clinic, and ran back to the river. When I arrived at the water, fear stopped me in my steps. I was afraid of getting back on the boat. Sakura might still be awake, awaiting my report. But I hadn't worked up the courage to report what I'd witnessed.

I walked past the boat and headed toward the shack under the bridge. I wanted to shut myself up inside for a while to think through my feelings. If I wasn't home when Father and Shosuke returned, they would probably look for me in the shack. So, even if I fell asleep inside, I wouldn't make them worry too much.

やがて清子さんと鉢合わせした。

（あら和ちゃん、小屋に行くの）

問われ、近付いていくと、湯を浴びてきた人独特の、なんとも言えない良い香りが漂ってきた。

僕の表情の変化に気付いたのか、彼女は急に態度を変え、（なに。お父さんに告げ口でもする？　お前がどうやって？）とせせら笑った。

桜を抱きたがる旦那も後を絶たないが、それは清子さんにしても同じだった。

彼女がこっそりと彼らに声をかけ、陰で身をひさいでいるのに気付いたお父さんは、二度三度、激しい調子で彼女を叱責した。

でも清子さんはやめない。お金が好きなのだ。それこそくだんが買えそうなほどたくさんのお金を、草陰で嬉しそうに数えているのを見たことがある。ふだんどこに隠しているのかは、誰も知らない。

僕らはいったん離れたが、（ちょっと和ちゃん）とまた呼び止められた。（ちょっとこっち向きなさい。お向きなさい。聞こえてる？）

僕は振り返り、頷いた。

70

I bumped into Kiyoko on the way.

"It's you, Kazu-chan. Are you going to the shack?"

As I approached her, the fresh scent of recently bathed skin wafted toward me.

When she noticed a change in my expression, her attitude took a sudden turn. "Are you gonna rat me out?" she smirked.

Our patrons lined up for and lusted after not only Sakura, but also Kiyoko. Once, when Father noticed she was arranging trysts, he gave her a stern talking-to.

But Kiyoko loved money too much to stop. Once I saw her gleefully counting her money among the tall grass. No one knew where she usually kept her money.

I moved away from her, but she called to me again. "Kazu-chan, turn around. Can you hear me?"

I obeyed and nodded.

（今は私を莫迦にしているがいいよ。でも私がこうして必死に稼いでいるのは、お前を聾学校にやるお金だからね）

弟分に侮られまいとしての口から出任せだったのかもしれないが、ともかく彼女が発してきた言葉のうち、これほどまでに僕を唖然とさせたものはなかった。

（たぶん家族のなかで、お前がいちばん頭がいい。だからご時世が変わったら、お前は学校に行くんだよ、私が貯めたお金で）

僕はかぶりを振った。よりによってその晩だ。お前も舟を降りろと言われているようにしか感じなかった。冗談ではなかった。

（どうせその時は来る。そのときじっくりと考えてみるがいい、自分の頭でね。お父さんだって、きっと長くはないんだから）

いっそう強くかぶりを振って、僕は小屋へと駆けた。そして翌朝兄さんが探しにくるまで、そのなかで踞って眠っていた。

（俺やお父さんに放っとかれて、ふて腐れてたのか？　あのあと酒をご馳走になって、蒲団で寝かせてもらったんだよ。お父さんもそうしろって）

兄さんはすまなそうに言い訳したが、べつに羨ましくはなかった。家族が揃った舟の上のほうが寝心地がいいに決まっている。

74

"You can despise me all you want. But I'm working hard and saving money so I can send you to a school for the deaf."

Maybe that was nonsense that had popped into her mind, but her words stunned me more than anything she'd uttered before.

"You're the smartest one in the family. So, when things change, you're going to school."

I shook my head. I felt like she was telling me to get off the boat. She wasn't joking.

"That time will come. I want you to seriously consider it. Father won't be here much longer."

I shook my head harder and dashed into the shack. I slept until Shosuke came looking for me in the morning.

"Were you sulking because we didn't come home last night? The doctor served us drinks and asked us to stay. Father agreed."

Shosuke seemed apologetic, but I didn't envy him, in fact. It was much more comfortable to sleep on the boat with the whole family.

陽の下に出てしばらくしてから、五十回めの夢をみなかったことに気が付いた。

犬飼先生は頻繁にお父さんを連れ出すようになった。お父さんのほうも億劫がらなかったし、酒にありつきたい昭助兄さんに至っては、お伴が楽しみでならない様子だった。

ふたりが帰ってくるたび、僕と桜は怖々とお父さんのふるまいや顔色を窺っては、出掛ける前と変わりないかどうかを討議した。しかし、たぶん変わっていない、という確証のない期待ぶくみの結論に至るばかりだった。念のため、兄さんに変化がないかどうかも僕らは観察していた。こちらはお父さん以上に、まったく変わるところなく見えた。

いま何が起きているのかを兄さんと清子さんに伝えるべく、僕と桜はそのための手段を検討した。ふたりとも喋れないし、読み書きもできない。読み書きを学びたくとも、人にそう伝えるすべを持たない。

しかし僕には絵が描ける。足の指で筆を握れば、そればかりはそんじょそこらの手のある人々より、遥かに上手いという自負があった。桜は耳が聞える。僕とは違い、音による会話とはどういったものなのか、想像ではなく事実として知っている。真似をする余地がある。

「できるとは思えない」と桜は及び腰だった。

76

When I went outside, the sun was already high in the sky and it dawned on me that I hadn't had the same dream for the fiftieth time.

Dr. Inukai often came to take Father out. Father was quite willing, and Shosuke seemed to look forward to accompanying Father because he loved booze.

Every time they came home, Sakura and I observed Father's behavior and expressions and discussed whether or not he was still the same man. Every time we reached the wishful conclusion that he hadn't changed. We also observed Shosuke, but he showed no signs of being different.

Sakura and I also considered ways to tell Shosuke and Kiyoko what was happening. Neither of us could speak, read, or write. We wanted to learn to read and write, but we had no means to tell that to someone else.

Even so, I could draw. With a brush between my toes, I could draw better than anyone I knew. Sakura could hear. Unlike me, she knew what a conversation sounded like. I was sure she could learn to talk. But she seemed to have given up hope.

「自分でも何度も試してきた。でも私の舌はほかの人たちのようには動かない。

動かし方が分からない」

昭助兄さんや僕のように、清子さんのように、たんに特別に生まれついたというのではなく、二人として生まれたあとで半分にされてしまった桜には、生来無いところをほかが勝手に補ってしまうような、いわば野生の逞しさがない。蛙を呑もうが彫り物を入れようが、それらは見世物の蛇女を補うだけのものであって、桜を補ってきたわけではなかった。

彼女の賛同を待たずに、僕は小屋に籠もっては、不要な板きれに絵を描くようになった。海原に浮かぶ僕らの舟。近付いてくる別の舟。それに移るお父さん。夢の情景を幾つにも分けて描いて、かつて昭助兄さんに連れられて遠くから眺めた、紙芝居のようなものに仕立てようとしていた。

桜の決意を僕がじかに聞くことはなかったが、彼女なり陰での努力を始めていることは、家族が喋っているさまを見つめる、そのまなざしから明らかだった。

ある夕方、兄さんと僕が河原で炊事をしているとき、おもむろに舟から降りてきて、

「聞いていて」と僕に呼びかけた。

"I've tried many times. But my tongue doesn't move like it's supposed to. I don't know how to move it."

Unlike the rest of us, Sakura wasn't merely born different. After she lost her twin, which was half of her, she came to expect others to fill that void. She lacked the innate strength to be her own woman. Even though she swallowed frogs and showed off her tattooed skin on stage, these things were mere props to enhance her performance as a snake woman. They didn't boost Sakura's off-stage confidence.

Without her approval, I cooped myself up in the shed and drew pictures on pieces of wood. Our boat floating on the ocean. Another boat approaching us. Father getting on that other boat. I drew several scenes of my dream to make a kamishibai, like the one Shosuke had taken me to watch from afar.

Sakura never expressed her determination to learn to speak, but I could tell she was making an effort by observing how our family members talked to one other. One evening, while Shosuke and I were preparing dinner on the riverbank, Sakura came down from the boat.

"Listen," she said to me.

（どうした桜。腹でも痛いのか）と兄さんが心配して尋ねる。

それほどに、桜は緊張で青ざめていた。ひょっこひょっこと僕らの近くまで来ると、振り返って舟を指差して、（舟）と言った。

どの程度の出来映えだったのか、僕にはそれを知るすべがない。兄さんはきょとんとしていた。桜の顔に落胆の色がひろがる。俯く。そのうち兄さんは、なにか思い出したような素振りで舟に戻ってしまった。僕と桜は河原に取り残された。

桜は泣きはじめた。

奇妙に長い静寂のあと、（桜）という呼びかけに顔をあげると、お父さんを背負った兄さんが、舟から降りかけていた。

後ろに清子さんもいた。（桜、喋ったんだって？）

（舟と言ったよ。言ったよな？　お父さんにも聞かせてあげてくれ）

そう明るく兄さんに促されて、桜はかろうじて気をとりなおし、やがて再び、浮き世の言葉を発したのだった。

（舟）と。

秘かな練習の成果は、それだけではなかった。次いでお父さんを指差して（お父さん）と言った。

"What's the matter, Sakura?" Shosuke asked, worried. "Does your stomach hurt?"

Sakura looked ill and nervous. She walked with unsteady steps toward us, turned, and pointed to the boat.

"Boat," she said.

I had no idea how well she spoke. Shosuke looked dazed. A look of disappointment spread across Sakura's face, and she hung her head. A short while later, Shosuke went back to the boat as if he had some business to take care of, leaving us alone on the riverbank. Sakura burst into tears.

After a long, eerie silence, a voice called to Sakura. When I looked up, I saw Shosuke get off the boat, carrying Father on his back. Kiyoko followed close behind.

"Sakura, did you just speak?" she asked.

"You said 'boat,' didn't you? Say it to Father." Shosuke cheerfully urged Sakura.

Sakura managed to bounce back and said, "Boat."

That wasn't the only fruit of her efforts. She pointed to Father and said, "Father."

（お父さん、聞えたかい）

（うん、聞えた）

（俺は？　俺は？）

（昭助さん）と桜は言い、さらに清子さんと僕とを続けて指しながら、（清子さ

ん、和郎さん）

兄さんはお父さんを背負ったまま小躍りした。（この人は？）

（お父さん）

（俺は？）

（昭助さん）

（この人は？）

（清子さん）

（あいつは？）

（和郎さん）

（あれは？）

（舟）

"Father, did you hear that?"

"Yes, I did."

"And me?"

"Shosuke." Sakura pointed to Kiyoko and me and said, "Kiyoko. Kazuo."

Shosuke jumped for joy. "Who is this?"

"Father."

"Me?"

"Shosuke."

"Who is this?"

"Kiyoko."

"Him?"

"Kazuo"

"What's that?"

"Boat."

調子に乗った兄さんは、空や対岸や河原の上のあちこちを指しては（あれは？）（これは？）とも尋ねたが、桜は笑いながらかぶりを振った。最初は、五つだけだった。お父さん。昭助さん。清子さん。和郎さん。舟。

他方、僕の制作も順調だった。絵具の種類が乏しかったため彩色には不満足ながら、細長い板二枚続きの、ちょっとした絵物語のていを成すに至っていた。まず桜に見せると、彼女の夢もおおむねその通りだったと言う。

僕らは小屋に昭助兄さんを招いた。絵を見せた。

兄さんは僕の画力を称賛してくれた。桜が絵に指を添えては言葉を発するたび、彼女の頭を撫でたり抱き締めたりもした。しかし残念ながら、僕らの本来の目的は果たしえなかった。兄さんは僕らの一連の行動を、新しい遊びとしか捉えてくれなかった。単語を羅列するばかりの桜の言語能力は、煩瑣な概念の説明にはあまりにも不向きだったのだ。

86

Shosuke got carried away and kept pointing to various objects in the sky, on the opposite shore, and on the riverbank, asking Sakura what they were. She shook her head, smiling. So far she'd learned to say only five words: Father, Shosuke, Kiyoko, Kazuo, and boat.

Meanwhile, my picture came along smoothly. I didn't have a wide variety of paints, so the colors failed to satisfy me. But my illustrated story eventually grew to consist of two elongated plates. When I showed them to Sakura, she thought they more or less matched her dream.

We invited Shosuke into the shed and showed him the picture.

He praised my painting skills. As Sakura pointed to the picture and uttered a word, he stroked her head and embraced her. But sadly, he failed to understand the true purpose behind the picture. He only thought we were playing a new game. Sakura's linguistic abilities allowed her to rattle off a string of words, but were still inadequate to explain complicated concepts.

彼女は癪癪を起こし、また泣きはじめた。絵が拙いせいだと僕は彼女を慰め、描き直しを約束した。

約束が果たされるときは訪れなかった。

その夕方、また犬飼先生がやって来たのだ。少なくとも僕の認識においては。

（岩国ではすまなかった。くだんは補給廠にいるよ。さあ、みんなで会いにいこう。それが君らのお父さんの希望だ）と。

ぞろぞろと土手を上がっていく途中、例の、不意に呼びかけられたような感覚があって、僕は河のほうを振り向いた。しかし眼下にひろがっているのは、草が揺れ、河面が揺れ、僕らの舟がゆったりと上下しているだけの、普段と変わらぬ景色だった。

繕いものが得意な清子さんが、薄い箇所を見つけては新しい布を縫いつけてきた雨除けが、強い夕陽に照らされ、戦争がひどくなる前に物陰から覗いたことしかない縁日の参道のような、なんとも言えない色彩の饗宴をなしていた。自分が最も満たされた気持ちにつつまれるのは、この土手からあの舟を見下ろすときだったことを、僕はあらためて思い出した。

Sakura lost her temper and began to cry. I consoled her while blaming my crude painting and promised her I'd paint another one.

I never had a chance to keep my promise.

That evening, Dr. Inukai paid us another visit. He gathered all of us below deck.

"I'm sorry for what happened in Iwakuni. The kudan is in the ordnance depot. Let's go see it. That's what your father wants."

As we climbed up the embankment one after the other, I felt someone call me suddenly. I turned toward the river, but the landscape before me remained the same: the grass swaying in the wind, the water's surface shimmering, and our boat floating up and down.

The patched tarpaulin Kiyoko had mended with different cloths created a feast of colors in the evening sunlight, reminding me of a path lined with stalls on a festival day that I'd seen only from a distance. I remembered I felt most fulfilled when I gazed down on the boat from this embankment.

* * *

犬飼医院で、先生とその腹心らしい若い兵士の手により、僕らは輸送用の木箱一つに詰め込まれた。お父さんと僕に腕や脚が無く、昭助兄さんは一寸法師、桜も最初から体が曲がっているから、辛うじて入れたようなもので、犬飼先生とその家族だったら二人で限界だったろう。

肌という肌がすべて家族と密着しているような状態で、持ち上げられ、落とされ、横倒され、また横倒され、延々と揺さぶられ、落とされ、揺られ、また落とされ、長いこと待たされ……ようやく僕らは釘抜きの音を聞いた。箱の一方が開き、僕らは外に這い出た。さっきまで一つの肉塊のようだったのが、五つの肉体へと戻った。

はじめ戸外かと思ったのだが、塀だと感じていたものを見上げていくと、ずいぶんな高さに天井の梁があった。あちこちに大量の木箱が積まれている。全貌が分からないほど広大な倉庫の片隅に、僕らはいた。

いっそう隅に、まるで僕らが興行のために建てるような掘建てがあり、その周囲にだけ電灯が点っていた。

（窮屈な思いをさせたね。くだんはあのなかだ）と先生が僕らに言った。（そろそろ夜が冷えてくるし、それなりに臭いもあるんで、急拵えしたんだよ）

Once we arrived at the clinic, Dr. Inukai and a young soldier, who served as the doctor's right-hand man, placed us into a wooden crate. Father and I lacked limbs, Shosuke was an issun-boshi, and Sakura had a crooked body, so we managed to fit inside. Otherwise, the crate was barely large enough for two adults.

We were stuck together inside like sardines in a can. The crate was lifted, dropped, tipped, flipped, shaken for a long time, dropped, shaken, and dropped again. After that, we were left alone for a while before we heard the nails being removed. When one side of the crate opened, we crawled out like one lump of flesh splitting into five bodies.

At first, I thought I was outside. But as I looked up at what I'd thought was a fence, I realized there were ceiling beams high above our heads. Wooden crates were piled up everywhere. We were in an enormous warehouse.

In the far corner, there was a shack like the one we built to perform, surrounded by lights.

"Sorry about the uncomfortable trip," the doctor said. "The kudan is over there. It gets cold at night, and it also smells, so we had to improvise the shack."

肌という肌が

すべて家族も

着しているような状態で

持ち上げられ、

お、た、横倒き流

兵士が筵（むしろ）をまくり、その次の覆いもまくって電灯を点す。柵の向こうにくだんがいた。膝を折って薬の上に寝そべっていた。想像していたよりずっと大きかった。体も、顔も。

人の顔をしているとは、僕は感じなかった。赤い、鬼の面に似ていた。褐色の毛皮を割るように、それが肩の下ににゅっと生えているさまは不気味だったが、必ずしも恐ろしくはなかった。眠たげに瞼（まぶた）を動かしている大きな眼と、固くむすばれた口許が、一切を諦めているような静けさを湛えていた。

（話をしても？）

お父さんが先生に問い、先生も頷いたが、

（お久し振り）と、くだんのほうがさきに挨拶してきた。低く深い声だった。

（岩国でお会いして以来ですね）

（私たちを見ていたのか。憶えているのか）とお父さんが驚く。

（トラックの荷台の、被いの隙間からお姿を拝見しました。どこへなりとお連れしましょう。そして私は殺されましょう）

僕らは顔を見合わせた。

犬飼先生が問う。（誰がお前を殺すというのだ）

The soldier rolled up a woven mat, pushed away the cover, and turned on the lights. I spotted the kudan behind a fence. The kudan lay on straw, both of its front legs bent. Its body and face were larger than I'd imagined.

The kudan's face didn't look very human to me; it bore a resemblance to a red oni mask. It creeped me out to look into its face above its brown furred shoulders, but I wasn't frightened. Its heavy-lidded, sleepy eyes and firmly shut mouth emitted a serene air of resignation.

"May I talk to it?" Father asked, and the doctor nodded.

"Long time no see." The kudan spoke first in a low, deep voice. "We last met in Iwakuni."

"You saw us!" Father said, surprised. "You remember us!"

"I saw you through a gap in the tarpaulin covering the flatbed of the truck. I'll take you wherever you wish, and I'll be killed."

We looked at each other.

"Who's going to kill you?" Dr. Inukai asked.

くだんはかしらを巡らせ、（そちらの若い兵隊さんです。私のことを、戦意を喪失させるために敵国から送り込まれた兵器であると、本気で考えておられます）

（斐坂くん、事実か）

兵士はぎょっと目を見開いたまま、直立不動となった。

（本当にそういう腹積もりだったのか）先生が重ねて訊く。

すると兵士は震え声で、（僭越ながら、只今の弁も、我々の攪乱が目的かと）

（決して独断するな。くだんを殺してはならん。返事は？）

（はい）

（雪之助、くだんに問いたいことがあれば）先生はそこで言葉を選んだ。（手短に）

お父さんは昭助兄さんに指示して、自分をくだんに近付けさせた。（お前は真実しか語らないと聞いた）

（あえて嘘偽りを申し上げることはありません。そうすべき理由が私にはありませんから）

The kudan turned his head. "That young soldier. He believes I'm a weapon your enemies sent to destroy your will to fight."

"Isaka, is that true?"

The soldier froze with his eyes wide open.

"Were you going to kill the kudan?" Dr. Inukai asked.

"With all due respect, it's trying to confuse us," the soldier said in a trembling voice.

"Don't jump to conclusions. Don't kill the kudan. Is that understood?"

"Yes, Doctor."

"Yukinosuke, is there anything you want to ask the kudan?" The doctor paused and chose his words carefully. "Keep it short."

Father gestured for Shosuke to move him closer to the kudan.

"I've been told that you only tell the truth."

"I won't tell lies. I have no reason to."

（その言葉を信じて問おう。お前はなぜ、私たちをほかの世界に導こうとするんだい？）

（導こうという意図はありません。私はそういう装置であると、皆さんにご説明しているだけです）

（装置？　お前は機械なのか）

（いま問われました意味においては、機械ではなく生物です。しかし自然繁殖はしません。個体ごと人手によって生まれ、そして死にます）

（人の手で創られた生き物ということか）

（いかにも）

（それは未来での話かい）

（内海を巡回する航路があるとします。すると海上の一点は、船の前とも後ろともつきません。しかし私の生まれた座標が、ここからは未来と感じられやすい、というふうには申せましょう）

（それが歴史の姿なのか。ぐるぐると内海を巡るというのが）

"Then I'll believe you. Why do you want to take us to another world?"

"I have no intention of doing so. I'm just telling you I'm designed to do so."

"Designed? Are you a machine?"

"According to the meaning of your question, I'm a living creature. But I don't reproduce. I'm artificially created as an individual entity. I will die."

"You're a man-made creature."

"That's correct."

"Are you talking about the future?"

"Let's suppose you sail along a route through an inland sea. You discover there's a part of the water that you can't reach by traditional means. You might believe I'm born in the future based on the way you understand time now."

"Going around an inland sea. Is that what history looks like?"

（単純な円環とは限りませんが、どうあれ内海からは出られません。正確に言えば、外のことを私たちは感知できません。しかし航路は無数に存在します。その

さまを俯瞰し、意図的な乗換えをおこなうための装置が、私です）

（未来の人々が自分たちのためにお前を拵えたのだとしたら、なぜお前は私たちの前に現れ、今も留まっているんだろう）

（私は最初から海上の一点を漂っているに過ぎないのです。傍をさまざまな船が通過していきます）

（そのうちの一艘が、この私たちの歴史だというのだね）

（いかにも）

（凄まじい爆弾が落ちて、日本は負けると聞いた）

（この航路においては、その通りです）

（日本人は全滅かい）

（いいえ、全滅はしません）

（では）お父さんは大きく息をして、（ここにいる私たちのうち、いちばん早く死ぬのは誰だろう）

（犬飼先生です）

"It's not necessarily a simple ring. At any rate, you can't leave the inland sea. To be precise, I can't detect what's outside of it. But there are an infinite number of routes. I'm the device that looks down on the routes and is used to switch from one route to another."

"If future scientists created you for themselves, why do you appear before us and remain here?"

"I'm just drifting on the ocean of time. Many ships pass me by."

"One of the ships is our history?"

"Yes."

"I've heard tremendous bombs will be dropped. Japan will be forced to surrender."

"That's true on this route."

"Are we going to be annihilated?"

"No."

"Let me ask you, then." Father took a deep breath. "Who among us will die first?"

"Dr. Inukai."

お父さんは愕然と、先生のほうを向いた。

（心配するな）と先生が硬い表情で応じる。（黙っていたが、私もすでに別の世界に逃げている）

僕がまたくだんに視線を戻した瞬間、その額にぽっと穴が生じた。くだんが撃たれた。そう気付いて振り返ると、兵士が拳銃を握ったまま身を震わせていた。

（斐坂、貴様）

犬飼先生が摑みかからんばかりの勢いで迫り、ふと後ろざまにひっくり返った。先生も撃たれたのだ。昭助兄さんが慌ててお父さんを下ろして、兵士に体当たりする。兵士は掘建ての壁の一枚ごと吹っ飛ばされた。

（さあ参りましょう）と、くだんが落ち着きはらった調子で言う。（私はまだしばらく死にません）

（次は誰だ。次に死ぬのは）

（斐坂さんです。いま私を撃った兵隊さんです）

（次は）

（腕の無い坊ちゃんと、彫り物のお嬢さんです。同じ爆弾で）

Father gasped in astonishment and turned to him.

"Don't worry," Dr. Inukai said, a stern look on his face. "I didn't tell you, but I've already escaped to another world."

When I returned my gaze to the kudan, a hole appeared in its forehead. The kudan had been shot. When I turned, I saw the soldier holding his gun, his hands trembling.

"Isaka, how dare you!"

Dr. Inukai charged toward the soldier, threatening to grab him. Suddenly, he fell on his back, also from a gunshot. Shosuke hurriedly put Father down and threw his weight against the soldier. A wall collapsed along with the soldier.

"Let's go," the kudan said calmly. "I won't die for a while."

"Who's going to die next?" Father asked.

"Isaka—the soldier who shot me."

"Next?"

"The armless boy and the tattooed girl. By the same bomb."

（和郎、桜）お父さんは僕らを見上げ、切羽詰まった調子で、（行きなさい、急いで）

（本当は分かっているのですが、ご納得いただくため、その手続きとしてお尋ねします。おふたりをどういった世界にお連れしましょうか）

（和郎が学校に行けるところ）と清子さんが叫んだ。

（ふたりが長く幸せに生きられる世界だ。こんな要望でいいのかい）

「みんなも。ほかのみんなも幸せに！」と桜が叫ぶ。

（承りました。和郎さん、桜さん、背中にお乗りください）

予想外の展開に、僕は茫然自失していた。舟を乗り換えるのは、僕と桜だったのだ。

（行きなさい）

お父さんの強い命令に、僕はただ従うほかなかった。柵を乗り越え、くだんの背中に跨る。後ろに桜が乗った。

牛馬に乗った経験がなかったので、くだんが立ち上がったとき、ふっと意識が遠のくような感覚に襲われた。直後、尻の下が大きく揺れて、はたと我に返った。

くだんが倒れかけているのだと気付いて、咄嗟に藁の上へと飛び降りた。

"Kazuo, Sakura." Father looked up. "Go," he said, sounding desperate. "Hurry!"

"I know where we're going, but let me ask you a question so you can better understand. Where shall I take the two of you? What kind of world?"

"Somewhere Kazuo can go to school!" Kiyoko shouted.

"Somewhere they can live happily ever after. How about that?"

"All of you, I want all of you to be happy!" Sakura cried.

"All right then. Kazuo, Sakura, please get on my back."

I was stunned by this strange turn of events. Sakura and I were the ones who were changing boats.

"Go," Father said.

I had no choice but to follow his order. I stepped over the fence and mounted the kudan. Sakura followed suit, getting on behind me.

I'd never mounted an animal, so when the kudan stood, a dizzy spell hit me. But then I regained my senses when the kudan shook hard. Realizing the kudan was about to collapse, I leaped onto the straw.

くだんは前肢を折り、後肢も折った。横向きに、藁のなかへと身を沈めた。赤く大きな顔に僕は足を近付けてみたが、すでに呼吸していなかった。

（今ので、もう？）とお父さんは犬飼先生の許に蹙ったが、そちらもすでに息を引き取っているようだった。

兵士も、くだんの予言どおり掘建ての外で死んでいた。先生を強く慕ってきた兄さんが、怒りのあまり渾身の怪力で殴り続けたせいだ。

以後の、僕らが帰属してきた歴史は、誰しもご存じのとおりだ。恐らくは犬飼先生が兵器として開発中だった細菌に、補給廠を訪れた誰かが感染しており、軍の上層に謎の死病が蔓延した。戦闘不能に陥った日本は、余力を残しながらも連合国に無条件降伏、国土は長い占領時代へと入った。

のちにGHQの総司令官となる男が、厚木海軍飛行場に降り立った瞬間の写真は、日本国民をおおいに驚かせた。アメリカ極東軍の司令官時代、乗っていたボーイング機を日本の戦闘機群に撃ち落とされ九死に一生を得た彼は、片方の腕と片方の脚を完全に欠いていたのだ。

The kudan bent its forelegs and then its hind legs. It sank into the straw. When I stepped closer, I saw it wasn't breathing.

"That was it?" Father crawled toward Dr. Inukai, but the doctor lay lifeless.

As the kudan had prophesied, the soldier was dead. We found him outside the shack, pummeled by Shosuke's furious fists.

Everyone knew what happened next. A visitor to the ordnance depot got infected with the germ Dr. Inukai had been developing, and a mysterious plague spread among the military top brass. Unable to keep fighting, Japan surrendered unconditionally to the Allies, and its territory fell under long-term occupation.

The people of Japan were stunned to see a photo that captured the moment the future GHQ supreme commander descended the platform at the Naval Air Station at Atsugi. When he was Commander of the U.S. Army Forces in the Far East, his Boeing was shot down by Japanese fighters and he narrowly escaped death. He'd lost one arm and one leg.

にもかかわらず私怨を感じさせない彼の良心的な統治は、国民の絶大な支持を得た。チェコスロヴァキアの作家カレル・チャペックの愛読者でもあった彼は、同作家の戯曲に登場する人造人間の実現を確信しており、その意向は戦後の日本に、代替臓器、代替四肢の技術を花開かせる原動力となった。

僕たち一家には、うんざりするほどたくさんの大学や企業から、慈善の手が差し伸べられた。新技術に対する恰好の被験者の集まりだったからだ。

まず終戦五年めにして、お父さんが新しい両脚を得た。現在の代替肢と較べたらじつにお粗末、そのくせ維持にはやたらと手間のかかる代物だったが、そのお蔭で彼は余生において三度も、大きな舞台に立つことができた。

次に清子さんが新しい膝を得た。頭から角を取り去り、鼻の余計な穴も塞いだ彼女は、特別な経歴も手伝って新聞や雑誌に引っ張り凧となり、やがて映画にも出演した。

Even so, he seemed to hold no personal rancor, and his conscientious governance enjoyed overwhelming support among the Japanese. An avid reader of Czech writer Karel Čapek's work, he believed in the development of robots, and his advocacy helped artificial organ and limb technologies flourish in postwar Japan.

My family received an inordinate amount of attention from numerous universities and companies because we were ideal subjects for their new technologies.

Five years after the end of the war, Father obtained new legs. They paled in comparison to the prosthetic legs you can get nowadays and were a pain in the butt to maintain. But thanks to his new legs, Father was able to perform on the big stage three times before his death.

Kiyoko gained new knees. After she had her horns removed and her nose ring hole closed, her unique background helped propel her to celebrity status, and she began appearing in newspapers, magazines, and movies.

日進月歩の戦後医療も、昭助兄さんの背を伸ばす打出の小槌とはならなかった。

だけど技術が生まれていたとしても、兄さんは断固として断ったろう。日本に最初のプロレス団体が出来るや、すぐさまスカウトマンが彼の許を訪れていた。泣く子も黙る世紀の悪漢、ドワーフ昭助、誕生の瞬間だった。

僕と桜は、清子さんの出資で聾学校に通った。桜は聾者ではないが、話す技術を知らないということで生徒に相応しいと認められた。今の僕は二本の腕も得ている。しかし活用しているとは言いがたい。絵が仕事だ。細かい作業だ。新しい人工の指先が、使い慣れた足以上に役立つはずもない。日常の大概のことも、鍛えあげてきた足や歯や、あえて肩に残してもらった小さな指で事足りてしまう。僕が桜に新しい皮膚をという勧めも後を絶たなかったが、彼女は断り続けた。ただし背骨下絵を描いた彫り物に愛着があって、取り替える気がしないと言う。ただし背骨だけはまっすぐにしてもらった。

Ever-advancing medical technology in the postwar era still failed to help Shosuke grow in stature. Even if such technology had existed, he'd have turned it down. Once the first professional wrestling organization was formed in Japan, a scout came courting Shosuke. He made his ring debut as Dwarf Shosuke and was touted as the villain of the century.

Sakura and I went to a school for the deaf at Kiyoko's expense. Sakura wasn't deaf, but she was admitted to the school because she didn't know how to speak. By then I had two arms. But I didn't use them much. I made a living as a painter. New prosthetic fingers were useless compared to my toes. I could carry out most of my daily activities using my legs, teeth, and the little fingers on my shoulders.

Many people suggested Sakura get new skin, but she kept saying no. She was fond of the tattoo based on my drawing, so she didn't feel like changing it. But she did agree to have her backbone straightened.

お父さんとは死別、清子さんや昭助兄さんも今は離れて暮らしているけれど、桜と僕だけは一緒にいる。仲がいいときも悪いときもあるが、お互い自在に話せる相手と、簡単に離れられるものではない。

あの河原の近くに住んでいる。散歩で土手の上を通るたび、ふたりして僕らの舟が浮かんでいた場所を見下ろす。今の僕らの、最も幸福で、最もせつない時間だ。

心の置きどころの問題だと、犬飼先生はお父さんに解説していた。だとしたら、くだんは僕らを運びきれなかったに違いない。運びきる前に死んでしまったのだ。だって僕らの気持ちは相変わらず、あの悲惨な世界にある。僕と桜にとってはやがて爆弾によって終わってしまう、短く虚しい世界だったのかもしれないが、こちらのかりそめの自分が死んだら、また心はあそこに戻っていくという、確信めいた想いから僕らは逃れられずにいる。

色とりどりの襤褸（ぼろ）をまとった、あの美しい舟の上に。

Father passed away. Kiyoko and Shosuke lived somewhere else. But Sakura and I were still together. Sometimes we got along fine, and other times not so much. But we were inseparable, as she was the only one I could freely communicate with.

We still lived near the riverbank. Every time we walked along the embankment, we gazed down at the spot where the boat had been. These were both the happiest and saddest moments of our lives.

Dr. Inukai had told Father it was a matter of perspective. If that was true, the kudan had failed to carry us out of that world. It died while trying. That explained why our feelings stayed behind in that miserable world. It might have been a brief, futile world for Sakura and me because we succumbed to a bomb. Even so, I couldn't help but think my mind would return there once my temporal, physical life came to an end in this world.

We'd be back on that beautiful boat covered with colorful rags.

津原泰水 / Yasumi Tsuhara

小説家　1964年広島県生まれ。青山学院大学卒。1989年に少女小説家〈津原やすみ〉としてデビュー。1997年、〈津原泰水〉名義の長篇ホラーである『妖都』（早川書房）を発表。2011年の短篇集『11 eleven』が第2回Twitter文学賞国内部門第1位、収録作の「五色の舟」はSFマガジン「2014オールタイム・ベストSF」国内短篇部門第1位、また同作は近藤ようこにより漫画化され、第18回文化庁メディア芸術祭・マンガ部門大賞を受賞した。現在は、欧米や中国で作品が紹介されている。著書に『綺譚集』（東京創元社）、『11 eleven』（河出書房新社）『ブラバン』（新潮社）『バレエ・メカニック』（早川書房）、『歌うエスカルゴ』（角川春樹事務所）などがある。2022年10月2日逝去。

宇野亞喜良 / Aquirax Uno

1934年名古屋市生まれ。名古屋市立工芸高校図案科卒業。日本デザインセンター、スタジオ・イルフィルを経てフリー。日宣美特選、日宣美会員賞、講談社出版文化賞さしえ賞、サンリオ美術賞、赤い鳥さし絵賞、日本絵本賞、全広連日本宣伝賞山名賞、読売演劇大賞選考委員特別賞等を受賞。1999年紫綬褒章、2010年旭日小綬章受章。

Toshiya Kamei

おとぎ話や民話を題材に小説を執筆。短編を『Daily Science Fiction』や『Galaxy's Edge』など多くの雑誌に掲載。2021年、2022年に年刊傑作選『Best Asian Speculative Fiction』に選出。2021年、2022年にWriters of the Future コンテスト選外佳作。2022年に『Apex Magazine』主催マイクロフィクションコンテスト優勝。SFWA、Codex Writers' Group 会員。翻訳を『Clarkesworld』『The Magazine of Fantasy & Science Fiction』『Strange Horizons』などに寄稿。

Yasumi Tsuhara (1964-2022) was the author of numerous books, most recently the best-selling novel *Hikky Hikky Shake* (2019). He began publishing shōjo shōsetsu (girl's fiction) in 1989. In 1997, he made his debut in the horror genre with the acclaimed novel *Yōto*. His 2011 story collection *11* won the second Twitter Literary Award. In 2014, the manga adaptation of his story "Goshiki no fune" won the Bureau for Cultural Affairs' Media Arts Festival Grand Prize. English translations of his short stories have appeared in *Asymptote, Cherry Tree, Gargoyle Magazine, Storm Cellar*, and *The Valancourt Book of World Horror Stories, Vol. 2*.

Aquirax Uno born in Nagoya, Japan in 1934. He graduated from the Design Department of Nagoya City Industrial Arts High School. After working for Nippon Design Center and Studio Ilfil, Uno started doing freelance. Some of his accolades include the JAAC Special Award, JAAC Members Award, Kodansha Publishing Culture Awards for Illustration, Sanrio Art Award, Akai Tori Illustration Award, Japan Picture Book Award, JAF Japan Advertising Awards Yamana Prize, and Yomiuri Theater Awards Selection Committee Special Prize. In 1999, Uno received the Medal with Purple Ribbon. In 2010, he was awarded the Order of the Rising Sun, Gold Rays with Rosette.

Toshiya Kamei writes fiction inspired by fairy tales, folklore, and mythology. Their short stories have appeared in numerous magazines and anthologies, including *Daily Science Fiction* and *Galaxy's Edge*. Toshiya's short fiction was featured in the 2021 and 2022 editions of the anthology *Best Asian Speculative Fiction*. Since 2021, they have won multiple honorable mentions in the Writers of the Future Contest. In 2022, they won the Apex Microfiction Contest. Toshiya is a member of SFWA and Codex Writers. Their translations have appeared in *Clarkesworld, The Magazine of Fantasy & Science Fiction*, and *Strange Horizons*, among others.

編集部より

「ヴィジュアル版　五色の舟」ともいえる本書は、津原泰水さんが企画立案した書籍です。

津原さんからのご希望は二つ。

一、装画・挿画を宇野亞喜良さんにお願いしたい。

一、宇野さんの絵とともに海外の読者にも届けたいので、英訳を収録したい。翻訳はToshiya Kamei さんにお願いしたい。

具体的に企画がスタートしたのは二〇二一年七月のこと。二〇二二年六月二九日には、宇野さんの事務所へデザイナーの大島依提亜さんとともに訪れ、宇野さんの描かれたラフを前に二時間近く打ち合わせをいたしました。

二〇二二年一〇月二日、完成を前に、津原さんは亡くなりました。

この度、ご遺族、宇野亞喜良さん、大島依提亜さん、Toshiya Kamei さんをはじめ、多くの方々のお力により、本書が読者に届けられることを、なにより津原さんが喜ばれていると思います。

五色の舟
ごしきのふね

二〇二三年三月二〇日　初版印刷
二〇二三年三月三〇日　初版発行

著者　　　　　　津原泰水・作
　　　　　　　　宇野亞喜良・絵
　　　　　　　　Toshiya Kamei・英訳

ブックデザイン　大島依提亜

発行者　　　　　小野寺優

発行所　　　　　株式会社河出書房新社
　　　　　　　　一五一〇〇五一
　　　　　　　　東京都渋谷区千駄ヶ谷二―三二―二
　　　　　　　　電話　〇三―三四〇四―一二〇一［営業］
　　　　　　　　　　　〇三―三四〇四―八六一一［編集］
　　　　　　　　https://www.kawade.co.jp/

印刷　　　　　　凸版印刷株式会社
製本　　　　　　加藤製本株式会社

ISBN978-4-309-03099-9
Printed in Japan